SIGNS
for
SALE

By

MICHELE BENOIT SLAWSON

Illustrated by

BAGRAM IBATOULLINE

VIKING

VIKING

Published by the Penguin Group

Penguin Putnam Books for Young Readers, 345 Hudson Street, New York, New York 10014, U.S.A.

Penguin Books Ltd, 80 Strand, London WC2R 0RL, England

Penguin Books Australia Ltd, Ringwood, Victoria, Australia

Penguin Books Canada Ltd, 10 Alcorn Avenue, Toronto, Ontario, Canada M4V 3B2

Penguin Books (N.Z.) Ltd, 182-190 Wairau Road, Auckland 10, New Zealand

Penguin Books Ltd, Registered Offices: Harmondsworth, Middlesex, England

First published in 2002 by Viking, a division of Penguin Putnam Books for Young Readers.

1 3 5 7 9 10 8 6 4 2

LIBRARY OF CONGRESS CATALOGING-IN-PUBLICATION DATA

Slawson, Michele Benoit.

Signs For Sale / by Michele Benoit Slawson ; illustrated by Bagram Ibatoulline. p. cm.

Summary: While accompanying her father on the road one summer selling neon signs, a young girl makes a sale of her own.

ISBN 0-670-03568-8

[1. Selling—Fiction. 2. Fathers and daughters—Fiction. 3. Signs and signboards—Fiction.] I. Ibatoulline, Bagram, ill. II. Title.

PZ7.S63124 Si 2002 [E]—dc21 2001006110

Printed in Hong Kong
Set in Goudy Sans
Book design by Nancy Brennan

For Horatio again
— *M. B. S.*

For Maxim Kunin
— *B. I.*

"Imagine, if you will," Papa says, "our town as dark as midnight in the mountains with no hint of a moon. That's what it would be like without my signs."

And just like yesterday and all the days before yesterday, I close my eyes. I still can't imagine anything as dark as midnight in the mountains without the moon.

Papa is a traveling salesman. He sells signs, neon signs, the ones that light up a shop, a street, a whole town. This summer I am his helper. Someday I'm going to sell signs, too.

Every morning we pack up our convertible. In the trunk I store Papa's sketches of all our signs. He draws pictures from photos I take on earlier trips.

In the backseat we stack readerboard signs, our newest and hottest item. "These are selling like hotcakes," Papa says. "Mr. Hansen will go for one of these. They're not too big for his drugstore windows."

"And remember, they won't rob his wallet, either," I say.

Papa and I laugh, because Mr. Hansen says *all* signs will rob his wallet.

"I'm not saying he's cheap," Papa says, "but I'll bet he's got the first nickel he ever made."

Between us we keep our clipboard with a list of appointments. On top of that we have the camera and packs of gum to keep us going.

"I like the fruity flavors best," Papa says. "They sugar up the lips and make the sweet words flow."

That's when he becomes a real salesman. He puts on his sunglasses, rolls up the sleeves of his white shirt, and rests his arm on the car door.

"We're off!" he says.

Our first stop is Sophie's. Even though it's daytime, she's turned her sign on, and we can see the gold letters flashing OPHIE'S DINER.

"We can have the 'S' fixed next week, right?" I ask.

"You bet," Papa says.

We are just driving up when Sophie runs out her front door to meet us. "I hope you're here to sell a sign," she says. "I need another one. I need a sign with a hamburger with all the trimmings or an ice cream cone that sparkles like diamonds."

"Sophie, you've latched onto something good," Papa says as he steps from the car. "That's a sign that'll grab a hungry family right off the highway."

While Papa keeps talking, I'm snapping the diner from every angle. I want to see it just like the hungry family driving down the highway.

Sophie says I have enough photos to do a thousand sketches, and I'm going to wear myself out before the day has even started.

"How about some breakfast?" she asks, and she ties an apron around my waist. "I figure it this way; anyone who's big enough to sell signs is big enough to flip their own flapjacks." I'd rather take more pictures but I stop, 'cause Papa always says you've got to see it from the "buyer's eyeballs."

First, Sophie shows me how to turn the cakes when the bubbles appear. Then she does fancy wristwork and the pancakes do somersaults. She promises I can practice all the mornings we visit her. I promise *her* I'll be back every week this summer.

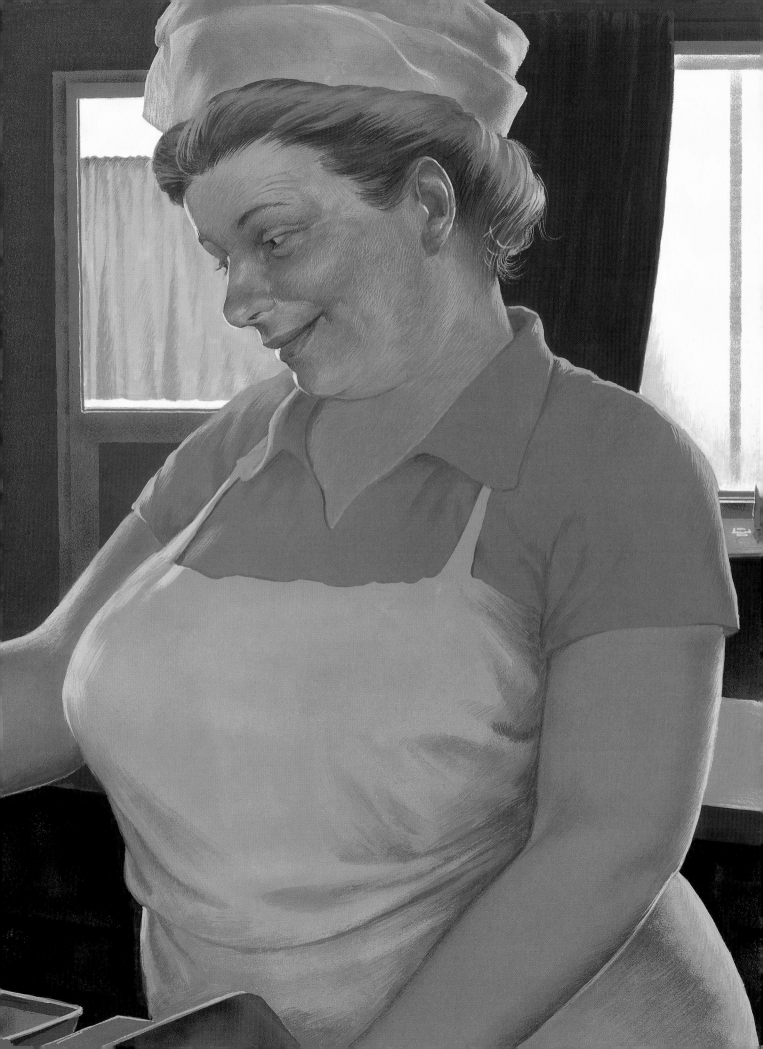

We jump back in the car, and Papa and I grab two new sticks of gum.

"Now we're rolling," Papa says.

"We're rolling big time," I say.

Our next stop is the Kellys. When we drive up, Dave and the sign company truck are already there. The whole Kelly family is waiting there, too. Papa told me they saved three years to buy this sign.

"These are real people," Papa says. "The real merchandise."

Dave asks everyone to move back, and the big crane lifts the new sign off the truck onto the roof. Dave climbs the ladder and makes sure the bolts are tight.

He gives the thumbs-up sign and Mrs. Kelly runs inside to flip the switch. KELLY'S MARKET lights up the sky!

Mr. Kelly hugs Mrs. Kelly and twirls her round and round. Amy, John, and Megan reach for each other, and everyone is hugging and kissing. That's when I snap their picture.

When we are back in the car, Papa turns to me. "See what I mean?" he says. "Real people, the gen-u-ine article."

Next is Mr. Hansen's drugstore. He's never bought a sign from Papa, so we don't waste a minute.

"I have just the ticket for you," Papa says. He grabs one of our readerboards from the backseat and pops in HANSEN'S DRUGS with orange letters. Mr. Hansen doesn't say anything. Papa is quiet, too, but his fingers are quick.

He trades the orange letters for red and green ones. Mr. Hansen doesn't say a word, so Papa plugs in the readerboard right in front of the store. Customers walk by and they notice Papa's sign. Papa switches the board on, and HAPPY HOLIDAYS lights up. Mr. Hansen's face lights up, too, but just a little.

"Probably costs a bundle of money," he says.

"That's the beauty of it," Papa says. "It's only twenty-five dollars."

"Too much," Mr. Hansen says.

Papa starts to take the letters off and pack up the readerboard like we're going home.

"Wait. You can mix and match the colors," I say. I open all the packets and fiddle with the orange, red, green, and blue letters. Now BIG SAVINGS lights up on the readerboard.

Mr. Hansen steps back to take a better look.

"I'll bet those letters cost extra," he says.

Papa winks at me, and I walk over to Mr. Hansen.

I stand on my tiptoes, and
I look him in the eye.

"You get it all," I say. "You get the readerboard sign that lights up *and* the packets of letters in a rainbow of colors for only twenty-five dollars. People really like this stuff, Mr. Hansen."

"Well, in that case you have yourselves a deal," he says, and he reaches for Papa's hand. Then he shakes mine, too!

After we are in our convertible Papa and I can't stop grinning. We both want to yell, but we don't. We wait and wait until we are sure Mr. Hansen can't hear us. Then Papa and I let out our loudest whistles ever. We honk the horn a hundred times. We sing all the way down the highway to the next town.

Papa reaches under the seat and hands me a new pair of sunglasses just like his, only my size.

"Congratulations on selling your first sign," he says. "That sign is gonna make him more money, every season of the year."

Papa helps me roll up my sleeves and waits until I rest my arm on the car door.

"We're off!" I say.

Papa and I are traveling salesmen. We sell signs, neon signs, the ones that light up a shop, a street, a whole town. Someday I'm going to sell a million signs.